D0408999

The Need for Speed

WITHDRAWN

adapted by Cordelia Evans
based on the screenplay written by Philippe Riche
illustrated by Shane L. Johnson

Ready-to-Read

Simon Spotlight
New York London Toronto Sydney New Delhi

SIMON SPOTLIGHT
An imprint of Simon & Schuster Children's Publishing Division
1230 Avenue of the Americas, New York, New York 10020
© 2014 Ubisoft Entertainment. All rights reserved. Rabbids, Ubisoft, and the Ubisoft logo are trademarks of Ubisoft Entertainment in the U.S. and/or other countries.
All rights reserved, including the right of reproduction in whole or in part in any form.
SIMON SPOTLIGHT, READY-TO-READ, and colophon are registered trademarks of Simon & Schuster, Inc.
For information about special discounts for bulk purchases, please contact Simon & Schuster Special Sales at 1-866-506-1949 or business@simonandschuster.com.
The Simon & Schuster Speakers Bureau can bring authors to your live event. For more information or to book an event contact the Simon & Schuster Speakers Bureau at 1-866-248-3049 or visit our website at www.simonspeakers.com.
Manufactured in the United States of America 0814 LAK
First Edition
2 4 6 8 10 9 7 5 3 1
ISBN 978-1-4814-2291-8 (pbk)
ISBN 978-1-4814-2292-5 (hc)
ISBN 978-1-4814-2293-2 (eBook)

CONTENTS

CHAPTER 1:
A Deserted Highway

A fly buzzed through the air down a deserted highway. Right behind the fly were four Rabbids. They were each hopping from one foot to the other down the middle of the road, because . . .

Why wouldn't they?

As the Rabbids continued their fun game (well, fun for them!), a police car drove past and pulled over. A young deputy named Garrett got out and dragged a heavy radar machine over to the side of the road.

"Deputy Garrett, report!" came a loud voice from the deputy's walkie-talkie. "I need photos of those license plates . . . and you better not mess this up!"

"Right, Chief!" Deputy Garrett said into the walkie-talkie. He went over to adjust the machine as a speeding van approached.

The Rabbids, who were now hopping over each other in the middle of the road, didn't notice the van approaching (or maybe they did notice it and didn't care). It sped past them so quickly that they were knocked over, right onto their butts.

Deputy Garrett's radar machine snapped a picture of the van.

"Yes!" he shouted, pumping his fist in the air. "You—are—mine!" he said to the van as it sped farther away into the distance.

But when he pulled the picture out of the radar machine, it did not show the license plate of the speeding van.

It showed a smiling Rabbid. (Why the Rabbid was smiling when it had just been knocked off its feet by a speeding van is unclear. But maybe being knocked over onto your butt is fun when you're a Rabbid!)

CHAPTER 2:
The Radar Machine

By now the Rabbids had noticed the radar machine. Of course, they didn't know it was a radar machine. All they knew was that it flashed, and then a picture of one of them came out of it!

Deputy Garrett's walkie-talkie chirped, and he tried to tell the chief what had happened, but he wasn't picking up a signal. So he walked away from the radar machine. Which, as you probably know, was not a very good idea.

The Rabbids surrounded the machine, pulling levers and pushing buttons . . . and there were a *lot* of buttons. Deputy Garrett finally noticed what they were doing and yelled at them to stop. But the Rabbids didn't want to stop, so they did something that made a lot of sense . . . to them, at least.

They picked up the radar machine and ran with it. In circles. Around the police car. Why would they do that, you might be wondering? Well, why not?

Deputy Garrett followed them around and around the police car, until one of the Rabbids decided the car itself was more interesting than the radar machine, and climbed inside.

The other Rabbids continued to lead Deputy Garrett in circles around the car.

The fourth Rabbid watched the action from inside the car, until he changed his mind and decided he wanted to be a part of the fun outside the car again. Or maybe it was getting really hot in the car. Either way, he opened the car door just as Deputy Garrett dashed around the corner, and knocked the deputy to the ground. On his butt.

"Bwooohhhh," said the Rabbids as they stared down at the deputy. Then the one in the car hopped out, stepped on Deputy Garrett, and they all ran off with the radar machine.

CHAPTER 3:
Bwuhhzz!

The Rabbids wanted the radar machine to take pictures of them again. They stood in front of it and looked at it very, very hard. But it still didn't flash the way it did when a car came by. This was because the Rabbids weren't tall enough for the machine to detect them, but they didn't know that, of course.

Then a fly came along and started buzzing around in front of the machine, which quickly began flashing and taking pictures. This gave the Rabbids an idea.

They decided to imitate the fly. They bwuhhzzed and bwahhzzed and flapped their arms in the air. They looked as much like flies as Rabbids can . . . which isn't very much, actually.

Still, the radar machine began taking pictures of the Rabbids! Well, it was really only taking pictures because the fly was flying in front of it, but the Rabbids *thought* they were the ones making it take pictures.

Three of the Rabbids were having so much fun pretending to be flies that they didn't even notice when the radar machine spat out the pictures it had taken of them. The fourth Rabbid, however, did notice. He took the pictures and stuck them onto Deputy Garrett's police car.

The other three Rabbids stopped playing. They all stood back and admired themselves.

They probably would have stood there admiring their images for very long time, but then the four Rabbids heard a strange noise.

It was the voice of the police chief coming from Deputy Garrett's walkie-talkie. The Rabbids went over to it and stared at it.

"Deputy Garrett! Are you there?" the walkie-talkie screeched.

One Rabbid picked up the walkie-talkie and tried to talk back to the police chief, but the chief couldn't hear him. The Rabbid didn't care. It was fun yelling into the screeching walkie-talkie! And he kept yelling until he realized he was upside down.

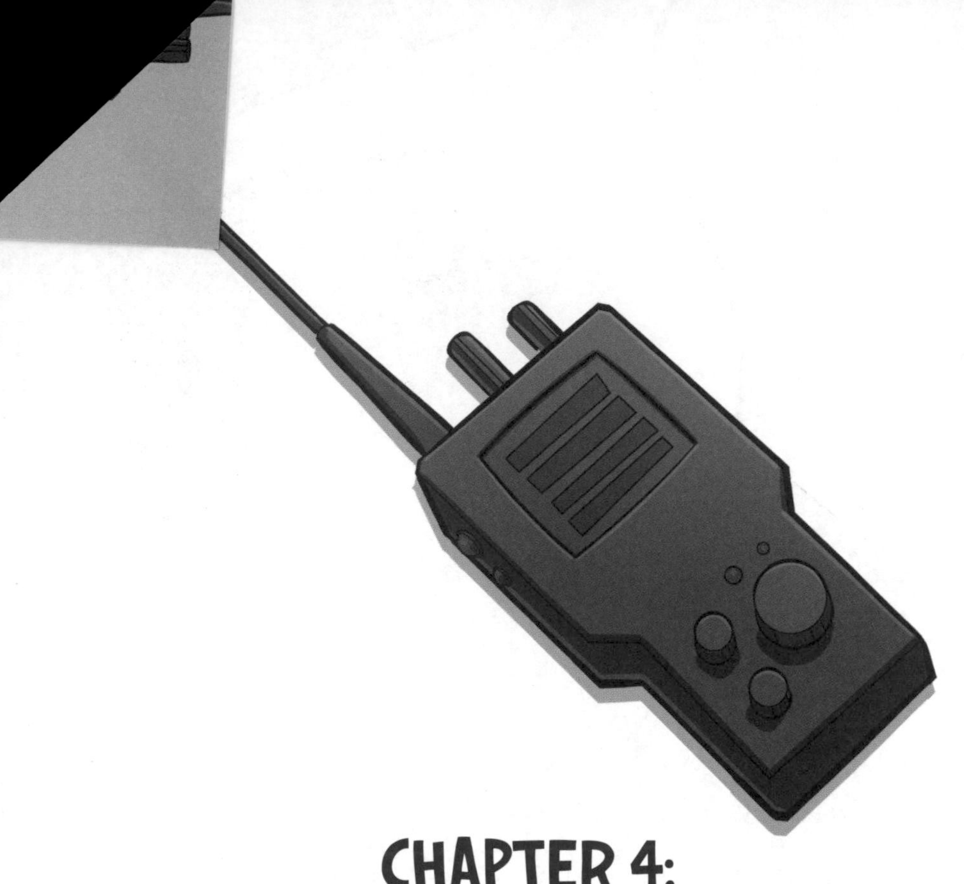

CHAPTER 4: Rabbids Take Flight

Deputy Garrett had woken up and picked up his walkie-talkie . . . with the Rabbid still attached to it. He shook the walkie-talkie hard, trying to get the Rabbid to let go, but the Rabbid would not. He may not have known what the walkie-talkie was and why a voice was coming out of it, but he knew he wanted it.

His Rabbid friends grabbed onto him to help get the walkie-talkie, but Deputy Garrett just pulled even harder. He pulled so hard that he launched all four Rabbids into the air.

“BWAAAAHHHH!” screamed the Rabbids as they soared through the sky. Then they decided that this flying thing was kind of fun! They flapped their arms but quickly realized that wasn’t going to stop them from falling.

And fall they did. All four Rabbids landed on the dusty ground with loud thuds. And yes, they landed on their butts.

CHAPTER 5:
To Catch a Rabbid

Now that he had gotten rid of the Rabbids (or so he thought), Deputy Garrett went back to his very important job of trying to catch speeding drivers. He reset his radar machine just as another car approached, and sure enough, the car was speeding.

This time, the picture that the machine spit out was actually of the car's license plate! Deputy Garrett was very happy.

Before the deputy could report his success back to the chief, another car came speeding by. This car was going faster than any car Deputy Garrett had ever seen! It went so fast that it knocked him over. (Can you guess how he landed?) His radar machine flashed and spit out a picture.

Deputy Garrett looked at the picture with a bad feeling. Sure enough, it was a picture of the Rabbids, hanging on to the back of a pickup truck as if they were surfing.

The Rabbids tried lots of different ways to have their picture taken by the radar machine.

Two Rabbids raced past on the insides of giant truck tires.

Two more Rabbids went by riding a big cow.

Another Rabbid rode by on a skateboard that was being pulled along by a tiny, fluffy dog.

Then one of the Rabbids went past riding a chicken. (If you're familiar with the Rabbids, then you know they *love* to ride chickens!)

Deputy Garrett tried his best to catch a Rabbid, but they slipped out of his grasp every time. Also, he focused on only one of the Rabbids, the one that was running in circles around the radar machine. It might have been easier to catch, say, one of the Rabbids riding the cow, because the cow was going very slowly . . . but poor Deputy Garrett wasn't thinking very clearly at this point.

In fact, the deputy was getting so fed up with the Rabbids that he grabbed the one thing he could catch: the radar machine. (The radar machine can't move, so obviously Deputy Garrett could catch it, but as we've said, he wasn't thinking very clearly.)

Then he took the radar machine and smashed it into pieces.

As you can imagine, the Rabbids loved this! They clapped along as the deputy jumped up and down on the machine.

CHAPTER 6:
Man Without Machine

Now that the deputy had destroyed his fancy radar machine, he was forced to use red and green paddles to tell cars when to stop and when to go. He stood at the crosswalk so he could tell pedestrians when it was safe to cross. There weren't really any pedestrians around though.

There were only Rabbids. Deputy Garrett sighed as the Rabbids waited patiently on the side of the highway for him to tell them when they could cross.

The Rabbids got halfway across the street before they stopped in their tracks. Can you guess what made them stop?

That's right, it was Deputy Garrett's red and green paddles that fascinated the Rabbids so much! They jumped and grabbed for the paddles until the deputy got so frustrated that he threw them on the ground and ran away screaming.

So the Rabbids were in control of directing traffic, and you can probably imagine how well that went.

Not well at all.

31901055934410